THE CURSE
OF
BEING PRETTY

(And Other Pitfalls...)

By Doraina Pyle

A special thanks to Mindy, Michelle, Dane & Al

Love to my family always

Cast of Characters
(in order of appearance)

Brian: The guy heavily into all things technology

Rooks: The quick-witted 34-year-old gal who shares equal passion for exercise and all things sugary

Michael: The waiter-next-door at Food Therapy, a comforting restaurant

Christian: The blond John Stamos of the apartment complex

Mom: The workaholic RN who shares a special bond with her baby girl

Granny: The meddling grandma, who is always heard but never seen... oddly enough

Elisa: The must-have-been-a-cheerleader-in-a-previous-life neighbor

Bruce: The big owner, operator, and boss of Bruce Levine's Advertizing Haven (BLAH)

Karen: The transient Office Manager of BLAH

Lindsay: The co-worker with surprising "true colors"

Graham: The other co-worker, a deemed sports fanatic with a California vibe

Denise: The free-spirited gal pal

Harper: The assertive, tell-it-like-it-is gal pal

Marley: The Mark Twain humorist of a gal pal

Rita: The hospital receptionist with definite two cents

Edith: The sadly-ill woman admitted into the hospital

Dad: The fanatical chess, baseball, and sugar daddi-o

Kirby: The overly-awkward neighbor across the street

Alex: The super obnoxious and superficial CEO

Andy: The snot of a friend to Elisa

Carie: The girl who wants to hook up with the snot of a friend to Elisa

Roger: The somewhat subdued fiancé

Steve: The guy who knows a little Shakespeare

Two businessmen: The men interested in advertizing assistance from BLAH

Susan: The waitress of one-liners at Food Therapy

SETTINGS

Food Therapy: No wonder this place is Rooks' favorite place to dine. With striped window awnings, rattan chairs, and cozy lighting, this bistro-styled, hole-in-the-wall restaurant serves the world's best comfort foods (such as pot pie, macaroni and cheese, and chicken and dumplings). Supposedly, the meals have fewer calories... except for maybe some of the desserts.

Outside the apartment: In a somewhat secluded, but open area, the buildings sit close together and are surrounded by green grass, trees, and sidewalk trails aplenty (perfect for jogging or walking dogs). The parking lot is at a reasonable distance from the complex.

Rooks' second-story apartment: Nerdy chic, if there is such a thing. There are wooden bookshelves filled with literature classics, pictures, and cutesy art décor, along with a mini-entertainment center that holds a TV and DVD collection of musicals, romantic comedies, and exercise videos. A couple of rook knick knacks are in sight. The treadmill is by the window, facing the TV. Directly behind the treadmill is a cushy recliner, and to the right of the recliner is an end table with a lamp and a few bookmarked books. There is a matching loveseat. Memorable family photos and inspiring art are on the walls. Overall the apartment is pretty clean, save an overflowing trashcan of diverse popsicle and candy wrappers; a recycling bin of water bottles, waffle cone boxes, and cool whip tubs; and shoes by the door. There is an open kitchen with a large countertop and sink next to the living room.

Bruce Levine's Advertizing Haven (BLAH): This is a private office that specializes in small-scale advertizing and printing. Services include, but are not limited to, brochures, fliers, copying, bulk copying, logo assistance and design, and online product promotion. Upon entry, there is a general reception area (decked to the nines in BLAH paraphernalia), and a hallway that leads to the Conference room and other offices in the back. The idea here: "controlled gaudiness."

The hospital: Two sets of automatic double doors open to a corridor that leads to a circular reception/nurse's station. The lobby is to the left. Behind the nurse's station are the hallways going to patients' rooms.

Rooks' parents' house: Set in a country, suburban neighborhood with the driveway in front of the house.

Rooks' parents' kitchen: Nothing says country like rooster ornamentation. The floor is tiled, and the kitchen table sits dead center. Usually, the chess board is atop the table alongside the rooster salt and pepper shakers. A picture of Ted Williams hangs on the wall. There is an open door to the side, where Granny often lurks...

Elisa's apartment and wedding venue: "If you want to catch a fellow, decorate your apartment in orange and yellow!" At least, that's what Elisa would say. She's got the walls of her apartment painted these festive colors with accents (like pillows and knick knacks) all-around (but not to the point of overwhelming). Quite the feat! The chapel and outdoor reception of her wedding parallel this same theme, with the addition of Chinese lanterns.

Rooks' car: A basic, run-of-the-mill vehicle with four doors and four wheels. Nothing too fancy.

THE SCENE BREAKdown

And so we commence our story...

SCENE 1 – Gotta Love That Technology

On their first date, Rooks and Brian are seated at a table at Food Therapy, Rooks' favorite small, but popular hole-in-the-wall restaurant.

Brian (*to Rooks as his cell phone rings*): Hey, can you hold on a second? I really need to take this. (*Picking his cell phone off the table and answering it*) Hello? Yes. Yes, I am. What news? Oh no way, you're kidding!

Michael, the waiter, comes over to the table.

Michael: Can I –

Brian shh-es Michael with his hand.

Brian: Unbelievable.

Michael (*whispering to Rooks*): Must be an important call.

Rooks (*deadpan*): Oh, it is. One Direction broke up.

Michael: Again? Blast that Zayn.[1] Can I get you something to drink? The usual?

Rooks: Water would be great.

Brian (*covering the receiver with his hand, he mouths*): Diet Coke.

Michael (*mouthing back*): What's that?

Brian (*confused, he mouths again*): Diet Coke.

Michael (*mouths*): Okay. (*Regular voice to Rooks*) And I'll get you your water.

Rooks (*smiling*): Thank you.

---

[1] #BecauseZaynLeft – The hashtag of devastation shared around the world when group member Zayn Malik announced he was leaving the band.

As Michael walks away, Brian finishes his call and puts his cell phone back on the table.

Brian: Okay. Now, where were we? Oh, yes. You were about to tell me about yourself, Rooks.

Rooks: Sure. Well, I'm –

Brian's phone buzzes with a text. He picks it up immediately, reads the text, and thumbs a reply.

Brian: Sorry. My friends wanted to know if I was on my date.

Rooks: And –

Brian: And I had to let them know that I was.

Rooks: But aren't they going to think it's sort of a lame date, if you're texting in the middle of it?

Brian: Oh, it's alright. They're cool. We do this all the time.

Rooks: You don't say?

Brian: So, you were telling – (*His phone rings again.*) Ope. Hold that thought. I've gotta take this. (*He gets up and walks to the restaurant corner.*) This is Brian.

Rooks gathers her belongings and gets up.

Michael (*with the water and Diet Coke*): You leaving?

Rooks: Might as well. Don't know that I could hold his attention unless I was implanted with a SIM card and an electric current.

Michael: Ouch. Sorry about that.

Rooks (*shrugging shoulders*): Eh. Who is John Galt?[2]

Michael: Want some cheesecake to go?

Rooks: Maybe tomorrow. Bye, Michael.

Michael: Bye.

---

[2] From the author's favorite book, *Atlas Shrugged* by Ayn Rand. Read it. Love it. Marry it. It is the best.

***

SCENE 2 – Chitty Chitty Chat Chat

With her phone stationed between her ear and her shoulder, Rooks gets out of her car, grabs her grocery bags, and walks up the sidewalk leading to her apartment. On the way, a handsome, sharply-dressed man passes, and she casually checks him out. She is still talking with her mom as she goes up the stairs and enters her apartment.

Mom: Where did you meet this guy again?

Rooks (*putting her groceries on the counter*): At the library.

Mom: And you were instantly attracted to his love of Tolstoy and telephones?

Rooks: I didn't realize he was an addict. I ran into him in the hallway near the bathroom.

Mom: Was he on the phone?

Rooks: Not at the time. I must have caught him between calls.

Mom: You need a better screening system.

Rooks: Like a Big Brother[3] monitoring device?

Mom: Something to that effect. There has to be a better way.

Granny (*in the background*): She got any old friends she could call?

Rooks (*matching volume*): My life is not a Nicholas Sparks[4] novel, Granny.

Mom: But the movies are so endearing.

Rooks: Only if Ryan Gosling[5] is standing in front of you in the rain.

---

[3] 1984 by George Orwell. Beware! Big Brother – or a drone – is watching you.
[4] Romantic author, known for his stories where former lovebirds reunite.
[5] As if anyone could forget that iconic scene from *The Notebook*!

Mom: It's not a bad thought, lovie. You had a few in there that had "Christmas movie[6]" potential.

Rooks: Oh, dear. You just air-quoted that, didn't you? Mom, it's been 15 years! Those ships have sailed. They're probably beach bums in Bermuda by now. Or Angola.

Granny (*in the background*): Well, is she doing all she can?

Rooks: Tell her the billboard went up yesterday.

Mom: Ooh. Is it the one near the park?

Rooks: It's over by the Wal-mart. I figured I'd get more traffic there. Save more.[7] Get a date.

Mom: She'll be thrilled.

There's a knock at Rooks' apartment door.

Rooks: Hold on, mom.

Rooks opens the door to find Elisa, her over-the-top enthusiastic neighbor.

Elisa: Oh, goodie! You're home. Oh, but wait! You are on the phone. Real quick, then. (*She hands Rooks a yellow paper.*) Roger and I are having a party in a few weeks, and we would love for you to come.

Rooks: Great. Need me to bring anything?

Elisa: Nope, we've got it covered. Just wanted to give you plenty of notice so you could mark your calendar!

Rooks: Thank you.

Elisa: See you there.

Rooks (*closing the door*): Bye. Okay, mom.

Mom: Elisa?

Rooks: Yeah. She's really sweet.

---

[6] Crazy enough, many a Christmas movie follows this same theme...
[7] Wal-Mart's customer promise. Dates not included.

Mom: Still set to marry her boyfriend?

Rooks: As far as I know. He is Emmett to her Elle.[8]

Mom: Hmmm… Maybe he has some friends?

Rooks: M-om!

Mom: Sorry, I was in granny-mode. You have met a lot of boys lately.

Rooks (*sighs*): It's true.

Mom: It's just that none of them match you.

Rooks: Also true. But I feel like I'm so far behind in the game. I should be married and have four kids by now. I should have something of a career.

Mom: Don't worry, lovie. It will happen. What do I always say?

Rooks (*thinking*): If you're going to sleep naked, keep a pair of pants by the bed?

Mom: It's only practical. What else?

Rooks: Always consider the jail time?

Mom: Very important to remember. And in this instance?

Rooks (*pausing*): Run your buns as best you can, and leave the rest up to the Man?

Mom: Ding ding ding. Tell her what she's won. Yes, the Man Upstairs will take care of everything – not always how we think He will, but He will. You've got to accept your life for what it is – not how it compares to everyone else's. No one reads from the same script. Now, enough preaching. I have an important question: When do I get to see you again?

Rooks: I don't know. Tomorrow?

---

[8] As in the "If there ever was a perfect couple, this one qualifies" musical adaptation of Legally Blonde.

Mom: Mmmmm…. That won't work, lovie. I've got two 12-hours on the schedule.

Rooks: Work, work, work… it's like I never see you.

Mom: I'm sorry, but you know I've got to work, if I want to retire with Howard Keel [9]– or your father. Besides, last I checked, you had a job too.

Rooks: Sure, throw that into the mix.

Mom: Shall we try for tomorrow evening?

Rooks: Can't. The girls are coming over.

Mom: So then we plan for soon?

Rooks: It's a date.

***

SCENE 3 – Au bureau

The four team members of Bruce Levine's Advertizing Haven (aka BLAH) – Karen, Graham, Lindsay, and Rooks – are seated already around a large table in the Conference room. Bruce, the head honcho, has scheduled a meeting.

Bruce (*entering*): Good morning, good morning, good morning! Glad to see everyone here. Shall we begin? (*Taking a seat*)

Everyone gives some sort of assent.

Bruce: We'd like to start today's meeting with a big announcement. Karen, I'll turn it over to you.

---

[9] His memory and baritone voice shall forever live on.

Karen (*standing*): Thank you, Bruce. First, let me say you are a great team. I know I demand a lot – I have always demanded a lot – but you've always delivered, no matter the request. Thank you. Thank you for being here, and thank you for living up to my expectations. Although I have known some of you longer than others (*looking at Rooks*), it has been wonderful working with all of you.

The team starts to exchange glances.

Bruce: Karen –

Karen (*taking a deep breath*): Right, the big announcement. Okay. There's not an easy way to say this… (*clearing throat*) So, okay, I'll just say it: My husband's family has been having some issues.

There is the typical feedback: "Oh no. Sorry to hear that."

Karen (*continuing*): Rather than go into all the details, let's just say that basically, it is better we be near them. (*She waits for understanding to register on the teams' faces.*) And so –

Rooks: Wait –

Lindsay: So this means –

Bruce: Karen is moving.

Karen: To Arizona.

Rooks: Arizona?

Graham: Whoa. Go Suns?[10]

Rooks (*with a sad face*): Woo-hoo?

There is silence.

Bruce (*standing up next to Karen*): I know this comes as a shock. Karen has done a tremendous job as Office Manager. We hate to see her go – especially since she has been here since the beginning of our little

---

[10] Phoenix's beloved team. Over here, it is Maverick fever all the way.

Advertizing Haven. But, we must push forward. There is still a tremendous amount of work to be done. Obviously, there will be changes. Let me mull things over, and I will have a game plan to you by the end of next week.

***

SCENE 4 – Cool Confrontations

Now that the secret is out, Karen has pulled boxes from hiding and is beginning to pack her neat little office.

Rooks (*knocking on Karen's office door*): So when's the big move?

Karen: I gave Bruce my two weeks' notice...

Rooks: How very Sandra Bullock[11] of you.

Karen: But...

Rooks: But?

Karen: But he said to go on with Elliot when he leaves. Next Friday is my last day.

Rooks: What? A week? That's not notice! What are we going to do without you? You are the peanutbutter and honey[12] that holds this office together. Everything rises and sets with you, Mrs. Molliker.

Karen: A job worth doing is worth doing well.[13]

Rooks: I agree.

Karen (*slyly*): And all is not lost, my young foodie.

---

[11] Such a quotable movie. "Did you say, 'Billy, I love you?'" "They said you weren't slurpee material."

[12] Add Cheerios, a dab of cinnamon, and sliced banana, and you've got yourself an amazing sandwich.

[13] Words of wisdom passed down from great-grandma.

Rooks: What do you mean by that?

Karen: Well, let's see. I seem to recall teaching you a few things over the last few months. Oh, yes, contracts, billing, case management.

Rooks: Et moi? I learned all that?

Karen: I have advised you on clientèle and given you difficult cases to handle.

Rooks: Was this your way of single-handedly trying to destroy my sanity?

Karen: Always a possibility. Or perhaps, it was my way of saying you could handle this job.

Rooks (*more serious*): What? Your job? You think so?

Karen: Absolutely. You are the best. No doubt he'll offer it to you.

Rooks: No.

Karen: Yes.

Rooks (*back to playful*): Then who will be fire monitor?

Karen: You'll have to turn in your vest.

Rooks: But I look good in orange.

Karen (*shooing her back to work*): You'll look good in this office too.

***

SCENE 5 – This Friday We GNI (Girl Nights In)

Rooks' three closest friends – Harper, Marley, and Denise – have come to her apartment bearing treats; that is, cinnamon rolls, baklava, cookies and pie.

Denise: Now this is a party.

Harper: You know we like to celebrate in style.

Rooks (*opening the cinnamon rolls*): This is way too much. (*To Marley*)

Don't you think this is way too much?

Marley: It's not the Cherpumple.[14]

Harper: So don't question it. *Enjoy* it.

Denise: To career advancement.

Harper: A new office manager.

Denise: Here! Here!

They clink forks.

Rooks: I don't have it yet, ladies.

Harper: But you will. So why not count chickens[15]?

Denise takes her plate over to the window to sit in the cushy chair

behind the treadmill.

Denise: Oh, dear heavens. This pie is delish!

Harper: You are welcome.

Rooks (*cutting into the baklava*): I think I'll go Greek.

Marley (*who brought it*): Good choice.

Denise (*looking out the window*): Someone has a new neighbor.

The rest of the group walk briskly across the room, and one-by-one

their heads pop into the window. Outside, the handsome guy Rooks

saw previously is jogging.

Harper: Mmmm, now *he* is delish. What a handsome man!

Marley: He can be my neighbor.[16]

Denise: Amen, sista!

Rooks: Hello, you're all married! You've taken the plunge.

Harper: We've bought the cow?

---

[14] The new Thanksgiving delight: a three-layer cake with a cherry, pumpkin, and apple pie in each layer (respectively).

[15] ...before they hatch.

[16] What would Mr. Rogers say?

Rooks (*laughing*): Precisely.

Denise (*almost sing-songy*): Yeah, but you haven't.

Harper: Have you talked to him?

Denise: Given him your number?

Harper: Asked him to be your future baby's daddy?

Rooks: Because that's not awkward.

Harper: Hey, you've got to do something. Get his attention.

Rooks: With what? A moose call?

Marley: Try something a little louder.[17]

Denise: Or you could start small (*eyeing the treadmill*) and ask him to go jogging.

Rooks: Ah, yes, because if he jogs and I jog, then we must be soul mates. Ladies, it is not that simple.

Denise: Of course it is! Don't over think it.

Rooks: I'm not. Thirty and Flirty is not always easy – or fun, for that matter.

Harper: Don't you switch to pity party mode. This is not the time to become Ms. Bitter Beans. Trust me. We've all been there, remember?

Denise: So true.

Marley: Oh, the woes of dating.

Denise: The lack of commitment!

Harper: The unwanted advances! Remember that guy who used to write crazy letters and give them to my brother to give to me? Or the 13-hour date?

Denise: Mr. I-Can't -Do-Lunch-or-You-Will-Think-I'm-Serious?

Harper: The married man?

---

[17] If there is such a thing...

Denise: The guy whose dad drove over four hours to convince him to ask me out on a date? And then the fool still never asked.

Harper: Ooh, ooh. The guy who fell off a roof?

Rooks: Not that again.

Harper: Hey! You try getting pictures from a hospital bed. Not easy! The guy had to learn to re-walk.

Rooks: Fine, I concede.

Harper: Oh! And remember the one who freaked out after one date? Holy cow, Batman.

Denise: How about that Republican?

Harper: And the Democrat?

Both: Ugh.

Marley (*interrupting*): At least you all could find people! I was on the corner with a cardboard "Date Me, I give great hugs" and still couldn't get any takers. Who's 30 and never been on a real date?

Harper: Yeah, but thanks to the world of cyberspace...

Denise: Now you have Phil.

Marley: Now I have Phil.

Rooks: That's love.[18]

They all sigh.

Denise: It sure is.

Harper: Have you ever considered online?

Denise: You've Got Mail.[19]

Rooks (*making a face*): Uh...I don't know. Another Tom Hanks may be out there, but that just doesn't feel magical to me. No offense.

Marley: None taken.

---

[18] Eh? Gotta love those puns.

[19] Nothing like a Rom-Com where business rivals fall in love over email.

Harper: So Match won't be calling you for the commercial. That's okay. But you do need to be more open.

Rooks: I talk to people. I say yes.

Harper: You're picky.

Rooks: I'm selective.

Harper: To-may-to, to-mah-to. And look how far it's gotten you. All I'm saying is, maybe you don't have to go to Egypt to find your treasure.[20]

Rooks: But –

Denise (*interceding*): How about you join a club?

Marley: Like Dating Anonymous?

Rooks: More like Dysfunctional Daters.[21] Hello, my name is Rooks. I am 34 years old, and I have trouble dating.

They all laugh.

Denise: Okay, okay. No clubs.

Harper: How about you just talk to that handsome stranger (*motioning to the window*)?

Denise: Here, here!

Marley: I'll clink to that.

They clink forks once again.

---

[20] Unless, of course, you want to see the pyramids. "They're beautiful, aren't they?" Ah, the brilliance that is *The Alchemist*.

[21] Not sure if there's really an official club, but Melinda Hill wrote a few columns in The Huffington Post for those who struggle.

***

SCENE 6 – Bringing Soon to Pass

Rooks goes to the hospital to surprise her mother at work, since they can't seem to find any other time to see each other. In her hands, she has a bouquet of brightly colored flowers.

Rooks: Hey, Rita. I'm looking for mom.

Rita: Hey, sweet girl! Did you cut your hair?

Rooks: No. Just washed it.

Rita: I might have to try that. It looks pretty good.

Rooks: Thank you.

Rita: Your mama is down hall two with a new patient. Room 203.

Rooks walks to the room and finds the door cracked open. Inside her mother is sitting on the side of the bed, holding the hand of a patient who looks rather ill and is connected to several IVs and monitors. She knocks softly on the door.

Rooks: Hey, mama.

Her mom turns her head to the side, and the lady on the bed opens her eyes.

Mom: Hey, lovie.

Edith (*weakly*): Ah, someone has a Mini-me.[22] You must be Melinda's daughter.

Rooks: Her one and only. It's a lot of pressure.

Mom: But she does a good job (*taking Rooks' free hand*).

Edith: I see you brought flowers. I love flowers.

---

[22] Yeah, baby... from the ever-so-popular Austin Powers: The Spy who Shagged Me.

Rooks: I did. (*Her mom gives her a nod.*) I would love for you to have them.

Edith: Well, aren't you the nicest thing? (*laughing*) You sure your mother won't mind?

Mom: Not in the least, Mrs. J –

Edith: Edith.

Mom: Edith.

Edith: Then by all means. You can put them next to the ones my son brought me. (*Rooks puts them next to the others.*) Now, don't those complement each other perfectly?

Rooks: They do – like they were meant to be.

Edith: You know, my son is single… close to your age, too.

Rooks: Is that right?

Edith: He wants to be a doctor. Starts medical school in a couple of months. Thinks somehow he'll be able to save me.

Rooks: That's a lofty goal.

Edith: He's a great guy – a bit of a John Lennon[23] incarnate with a heart of gold. Would you like me to give him a call?

Rooks (*clearing throat*): No, that's alright.

Edith: Are you sure?

Mom (*interceding*): She's sure, but thank you, Edith. She likes to find them on her own – no outside help.

Edith: Well, let me know if you change your mind.

Rooks: I will. Thank you.

---

[23] *Imagine.* Need I say more?

***

SCENE 7 – Walk with me, like Mothers Do[24]

Rooks and her mother go into the hospital hallway to finish their conversation.

Rooks: Is she alright?

Mom: Edith? Not particularly, but we are going to do all we can to keep her comfy.

Rooks: She seems nice.

Mom: She is. And funny too. Shares DNA with Jack Benny.[25]

Rooks: Well![26]

Mom (*giving Rooks a huge hug*): You look good. A little skinny, but good. Keeping up with your exercise, I see. But have you been getting enough protein? Eating your vegetables?

Rooks: Sure – when they are dipped in honey.

Mom: Rooks.

Rooks: You know I can't help myself. Must. Have. Sugar.

Mom: You are your father's daughter more and more each day. Speaking of, are you going to run by the house?

Rooks: That was the plan.

Mom: Good girl. Just make sure he has his insulin before you slip him any treats.

Rooks: Why whatever do you mean?

Mom: Uh-huh. Just remember: I am everywhere.

---

[24] In Eurythmics fashion.
[25] Comedic genius, very popular in the 50s.
[26] Said Jack Benny style.

Rooks: My mother is God? How did I not know this?

Mom (*swatting her bottom*): Out-of-here, you. And thanks for coming by.

***

SCENE 8 – Sneak and Snack Attack

Rooks pulls into her parents' driveway and gets a white bakery box out of the car before walking up the driveway.

Dad (*Peeking out the door suspiciously*): You got the goods?

Rooks: Dad! Open the door! You know I do.

Dad: And you're sure your mother didn't follow you?

Rooks: Impossible to say for sure. After all, she is a female James Bond.[27]

Dad: Don't I know it.

Rooks: Dad! I left her at the hospital. (*Looking around for extra measure*) We're safe. (*Seeing the awkward neighbor by his bushes across the street*) Well, mostly.

Dad: Alright. Come in, but be very quiet. We don't want to wake Granny.

Her dad takes one last look outside the door. Also seeing the neighbor across the street, he gives a giant wave, and then goes inside.

Rooks: I bet she's alrea-

Dad: Don't you jinx us. Is that the stuff?

---

[27] Ian Fleming's famous "Shaken, not stirred" spy who could face off against the Dark Side and the Hunger Games tributes and probably still manage to survive.

He moves his chessboard off the kitchen table so she can set the box down.

Rooks: Yes, but mom wanted to make sure you –

Dad: Already took it.

Rooks: You have?

Dad: I have been waiting for this moment.

He opens the lid of the box to find a freshly-baked peach cobbler.

Dad: Oh, bless you, my child. I have taught you well.

Rooks (*getting plates out of the cabinet*): Shall we?

Dad: Absolutely. (*Finding the knife*) Now give me the haps.

Rooks: Excuse me?

Dad: The haps. Tell me what's going on.

Rooks: Dad, you totes don't have to use haps.[28]

Dad (*serving the cobbler*): I'm trying to be cool, keep with the in-crowd.

Rooks: You're already cool. Anyways, not much.

Dad (*taking a bite*): Mom mentioned a possible promotion?

Rooks: It's not definite. I find out next week. Karen thinks I'm a shoo-in.

Dad: That's my girl. What else? Can I hope for grandchildren this lifetime?

Rooks: Dad, you have grandchildren.

Dad: Who live in Montana! Might as well be Russia. It's all the same.

Rooks: Still working on that geography, huh?

Dad: My original question stands. Give me some hope. And remember, (*nodding toward the open door*) Granny may be listening.

Rooks: Dad, I've told you. I've got to find a guy first.

---

[28] Totes and haps: New slang for the vocabulary-driven wanting to stay in the "in-crowd" (like this padre).

Dad: Well, are you playing ball? Because you know, I could help you with that.

Rooks: No. No, thank you.

Dad: Come on!

Rooks: Everyone always wants to set me up. The answer is no. I can do this on my own.

Dad: So no grandchildren then, huh? Break my heart, why don't ya?

Rooks: Dad, please. It'll be alright. If it makes you feel better, I saw someone the other day.

Dad: You saw someone? You saw someone. Did your eyes meet from across the room?

Rooks: He walked past me in the parking lot.

Dad: Uh-huh. I see. So you didn't actually meet? You're falling for a man at face value? Honey, did we not learn anything from Frozen?[29]

Rooks: You've seen Frozen?

Dad: What? You think I live in a box?

Rooks: No, of course not. Well, sometimes. Maybe. Okay, so he's not quite a go, but I've got another date coming up.

Dad: Ooooh. Give me deets.[30] Does he sing and dance like your papa?

Rooks (*laughing*): He might sway from side to side. I don't know yet. I'll give you the skinny when I find out, Fred.[31]

---

[29] The Disney blockbuster that will forever have us singing "Let It Go"...
[30] = details. More "cool" vocab, in case you were wondering.
[31] As in Fred Astaire, the great dancer and singer.

***

SCENE 9 – Dress to Impress (Khakis Would Be Inappropriate for Bowling)

Rooks is back at her apartment. In anticipation of her date, she puts on a dress and a little bit of make-up. When finished, Rooks grabs her purse and locks her door. On the way to the car, she sees the cute guy coming her direction. This time, she manages a soft "Hi," and he gives her a nod of acknowledgment.   When she looks back, she finds him looking at her. He gives her a small smile. S-l-o-w—l-y, she gets into her car and leaves for her date.

***

SCENE 10 – I'd prefer Mr. Trebek

Once again, Rooks is at Food Therapy to meet her date. She waits at the entrance for him to arrive. After what feels like eternity, he pulls up in a fancy car, wearing a suit.

Rooks: Hey, you made it.

Alex: Of course I made it. We had a date. Don't you look pretty?

Rooks: Thank you.

The two enter the restaurant, where Michael greets them.

Michael: Welcome. How is everyone doing tonight?

Alex: We are fine.

Michael: Wonderful. Let me show you to a table.

He leads them to a table by the window.

Alex (*barely glancing at the table*): Do you have anything better?

Michael: What seems to be the problem, sir?

Alex: It's filthy.

Michael and Rooks look at an impeccable table, and then at each other.

Michael: Uh… well. Let me see what I can do. If you'll give me a moment.

Alex: Son, I don't have any moments. Time is of the essence.

Michael: Then please forgive me… Father. (*He walks away.*)

Alex: Do you know that guy?

Rooks: I've been here a few times.

Alex: I can tell.

Rooks: Huh?

Michael returns with a rag and wipes the table.

Michael: There you go, sir. Is this more to your liking?

Alex (*seating*): I suppose it will do.

Michael: Can I get you something to drink?

Alex (*before Rooks can answer*): Two Dr. Peppers. (*He starts to look at the menu; Michael raises his eyebrows.*)

Rooks: Actually, I'll have water with lemon, please. (*Michael nods and leaves to go get the drinks.*)

Alex (*closing the menu*): Well, I have had quite the day today, let me tell you. It started this morning, and it has been downhill ever since.

Rooks: Present company excepted, I hope?

Alex: Oh, sure. But I lost $17,000.

Rooks: You lost $17,000?

Alex: Yes, in the stock market. So you can see where I'm at, can't you? What a day!

Rooks: I —

Alex: Waiter! Waiter! (*snapping his fingers*) Never where he ought to be, I suppose. (*Michael comes carrying the drinks.*) We're ready to order.

Rooks (*opening the menu*): Actually, I need a few minutes.

Alex: But you said you've been here before, right? Just get what you always do.

Rooks: Um... okay. (*Rooks closes her menu and turns to Michael, who already knows what she is going to order.*) Slice of cheesecake, extra whipped cream.

Alex: You're kidding.

Rooks: I never kid about dessert.

Alex: Okay, but you can't have dessert for dinner.[32] That's ridiculous.

Rooks: Not in my world.

Alex: How about chicken? Do you like chicken? Of course you do. Who doesn't like chicken? Bring a chicken dish for the lady, and I'll have the best meat you've got.

Michael: Would you still like the cheesecake?

Rooks: Yes, please.

Alex: No. Trust me, you'll love the chicken.

Rooks: I'm sure I will.

Michael: Coming right up.

Michael takes the menus and leaves.

Alex: Alright. So where were we? Oh yes, would you like to ask me any questions?

Rooks: Uh...Is there something in particular you'd like me to ask?

---

[32] Millions would disagree. Or, perhaps, millions of children... plus me.

Alex: Oh, anything really – how much I make, what kind of car I drive, where I've been...

Rooks: Wouldn't you rather I wait until we have a dark room and a spotlight?[33]

Alex: Oh, come on now.

Rooks: I don't feel comfortable asking these questions.

Alex: It's alright. Ask me anything. Any question at all.

Rooks: Okay... What do you like to do for fun?

Alex (*looking disappointed*): Generally, I like to go driving. Get this: My car goes from 0 to 60 in 4.5 seconds.

Rooks: So Fast and Furious[34]... Is it a Toyota?

Alex (*incredulous*): No! How could you think – Wait, you're teasing, right? You saw my car when I pulled up. Yeah, it's a great car. Runs like a champ. Got a good deal on it, you know?

Rooks: Sure, sure.

Michael arrives with their food. He sets it on the table and gives Rooks a wink; her chicken has a dollop of whipped cream on top.

Michael: Everything look alright?

Alex: Absolut- (*seeing the whipped cream*) What on earth is that?

Rooks: It's perfect. Thank you.

Michael (*before Alex can speak*): Bon appétit.

Rooks (*cutting into the chicken and taking a bite*): So was there anything else I should know about you?

Alex: Of course! But let me ask you a question.

Rooks (*with chicken in her mouth*): You want to ask *me* a question?

---

[33] À la police interrogation.
[34] Such a popular movie series where cars drive fast... and furious.

Alex: Of course. But I'll cut right to the chase: What do you think about us?

Rooks (*swallowing, her silverware frozen*): Us? Us... as in you and me?

Alex: Naturally. What do you think?

Rooks: I haven't wrapped my head around the idea.

Alex: Really? Because the way I see it, I think we have potential.

Rooks: You and me?

Alex: Yes!

Rooks (*eyeing the cool whip on her chicken*): Are you sure? I mean, this is a first date.

Alex: Hey, we both have great bodies. Clearly, we'd make a killer couple, don't you think?

Rooks: Yes, clearly – if we strained the mud.

Alex: You don't think we could do well together?

Regaining motion sense, Rooks puts a spoonful of cool whip into her mouth.

Rooks: At this point, I can't say that I do.

Alex: Well, how about this? We'll go on another date – someplace more intimate – and we'll try again. I'll let you ride shotgun.

Rooks (*scraping every bit of whipped cream off of the chicken and putting it into her mouth*): Mmm. Oh, that is delicious. (*back to Alex*) As wonderful as that would be, I think I'm going to have to pass.

Alex (*a little angry*): You're kidding.

Rooks: No, I'm pretty serious.

Alex: Unbelievable. (*Practically yelling*) Waiter!

Michael (*running over*): Yes, sir?

Alex: We'll have the check now.

Michael: Are you sure? You've only just begun...[35]

Rooks shakes her head as in this-is-not-the-time-for-jokes style.

Alex: The check. Now.

Michael: Yes, sir.

Rooks: Wait, are you really leaving?

Alex: Of course. This is a wasted investment. (*Grabbing his coat*) I'll leave you to get that (*nodding to Michael, who has the check*).

Rooks: Excuse me?

Alex: I can only handle so many losses in one day.

He gets up and storms out.

Michael (*with the check*): What happened?

Rooks: I'm not sure, but I think he just broke up with me.

Michael: He did sound serious. I take it, then, that you are never ever ever getting back together?[36]

Rooks: I don't think so.

Michael (*pausing a moment*): Cheesecake?

Rooks: Yes, please.

***

SCENE 11 – MaMa! DaDa!

Rooks is sitting around the kitchen table with her parents.

Mom: And what of this one?

Rooks: I met him at a yoga class a few weeks ago. At the time, he seemed like a nice guy.

---

[35] The Carpenters will sing along.
[36] Shout-out to the one and only Tay-Tay.

Mom: Oh, lovie, lovie, lovie. Never trust a man post-savasana.[37]

Rooks: Well, I'm not going to meet anyone staying at home doing Richard Simmons[38] videos.

Mom: You still have that tape?

Rooks: Maybe... that's beside the point. You are always telling me to put myself out there and to give people a chance. This is me trying to do that.

Mom: The chance part – yes. Sometimes you overlook people. The putting yourself out there –that's more your granny –

Granny (*in the background*): What about me?

Mom: Nothing, mom! (*quietly*) Although she does have a point.

Dad: I say you move past it. Let it roll off your back.

Mom: Yes. Got any more dates?

Dad: I could set you up. Please let me set you up.

Granny (*in the background*): I know some people.

Mom: She doesn't want anyone from ICU.

Dad: Mine's not in ICU.

Granny (*in the background*): Love has no number.

Dad: Although mine is closer to your age.

Rooks: Thanks, everyone, but no more dates right now. I need to focus on career. Maybe I can finally get that working for me.

Mom: That's right. We've got a soon-to-be office manager in our midst.

Rooks: You think I'm ready?

Mom: You could organize a dumpster.

---

[37] The final, most relaxing phase of yoga practice. Your house could collapse, and all would be well, because your cares have all slipped away.
[38] Fun-loving exercise guru who instructs everyone to "Shake off those fat cells." Not that I would know or anything...

Dad: Or your grandmother's medicine cabinet.

Granny (*in the background*): I heard that.

Rooks: Such pleasant thoughts.

Mom: Hey, you never know when they'll come in handy.

***

SCENE 12 – This is Big! Big, Big, Big![39]

Once again, the team is assembled in the Conference room, this time poised and ready to hear Bruce's decision. Bruce enters with a big smile on his face.

Bruce: Good morning, everyone!

Everyone: Good morning.

Bruce: I hope you have had a lovely week! As you know, today is Karen's last day.

Karen: We'll have food delivered later.

Bruce: Indeed we will.

Graham: Excellent.

Bruce: Again, we are sad to see you go. You have been tremendous!

Karen: Thank you.

Bruce: No doubt the rest of you are anxious to know what will happen.

Everyone: Yes, yes, we are.

Bruce: After careful consideration – taking into account office dynamics and what we really need, etc, etc, etc[40] – I am pleased to announce we have a new office manager.

---

[39] As Oprah would say.
[40] Spoken differently than King Mongkut.

Rooks sits straighter in her chair.

Bruce: Ladies – and gentleman – as of today, (*pausing*) Lindsay is Bruce

Levine's Advertizing Haven's new office manager!

Graham: Congratulations!

Rooks is surprised but tries to recover.

Karen: Bruce –

Bruce: A round of applause.

Graham claps.

Karen: Bruce, can I talk –

Bruce: Graham, if you'll help Lindsay move her stuff from reception to

the back, that would be great. She'll be in Karen's old office.

Graham: Totally.

Rooks looks at Karen, who is also in disbelief.

Bruce (*continuing*): Also, I'm going to have you stay put where you are,

but Rooks, I want you to move out to the front.

Rooks: To the front? Am I being demoted?

Bruce: By no means. You, my dear, are going to be the new face of

our company!

Rooks: I beg your pardon?

Bruce: We need someone to represent this company – someone with

warmth, someone with the know how to recruit clients and make them

stay; a person who can take this business to the next level.

Rooks: And I'm your choice?

Bruce: Naturally. With your smile and expertise, it had to be you. Just

imagine. When clients walk through the door, you'll be the first person

they see. When they call, you'll be the first person they hear. In

essence, Rooks, you will be their first impression. Isn't that exciting?

Rooks: It is something.

Bruce: Tremendous! I knew you'd think so.

Bruce walks over to Lindsay and gives her a lingering hug. Karen comes over to Rooks and puts her hand on her shoulder.

***

SCENE 13 – O Consolation, Where Art Thou?

Rooks is at her desk with her head down.

Karen (*knocking on the door*): I'm sorry, kid.

Rooks (*head still down*): It's not your fault. I guess I'm not the right girl for the job after all.

Karen: But you are! You could take on a rabid dog[41] if you wanted. I don't know what Bruce is thinking.

Rooks: He's thinking Lindsay would make a terrific Office Manager …

Karen: … because of her "tremendous business savvy." His words. I'm thinking "tremendous measurements" may have been more at play.

Rooks: But he's married.

Karen: Unfortunately, kid, that's not always a guarantee.

Rooks lifts her head to look at Karen. There is a large red desk imprint on her forehead.

Rooks: So he wants me to be the face of the company?

Karen: Apparently, you're pretty genuine.

Rooks: At this moment, I'm pretty dumbfounded. He wants Lindsay? He wants Lindsay. Lindsay – the same girl who confused consultation with contract?

---

[41] Her and Atticus Finch (from *To Kill A Mockingbird*).

Karen: Heaven forbid we move further down the alphabet.

Rooks: I mean, I want to live off cheesecake – or maybe pie – but that doesn't mean it's right. How is she going to handle accounting? Or client issues? She's been answering phones the last two months, and most of the time, she transferred those calls to me.

Karen: I know. (*Pause*) But Bruce did have a suggestion...

Rooks: Which is?

Karen: You're not going to like it.

Rooks: That may be a gross understatement. Come on. Considering how I feel right now, it couldn't possibly get any worse.

Karen: You'd be surprised.

Rooks: Go on, hit me, baby...

Karen: One more time?[42] Alright. Prepare for the knockout. (*Another pause*) Bruce is proposing you train her.

Rooks (*mouth dropping open*): What?!?!

Karen: I told you.

Rooks (*anger rising, body lifting from chair*): Let me get this straight. Bruce wants me, who knows the job, who you've prepared for the job –

Karen: - who should've gotten the job –

Rooks: - to train the girl who can barely answer phones?

Karen: And doesn't deserve it? Yes. That's exactly what he wants.

Rooks (*sinking down, putting her head back on the desk*): This is horrible.

Karen: I agree. And unfortunately, I can't change his mind. I'm sorry, kid. I did the best I could. You might try talking to him yourself, and

---

[42] Britney's big smash that made us all re-visit the Catholic school girl ensemble.

see what happens. (*There is no response*.) Listen, I couldn't find a candy bar. So would you settle for a mint and a bottle of water?

Rooks: Do you even have to ask?

Rooks lifts both hands, and Karen puts the mint in one and the bottle into the other. She rubs Rooks' back, and then walks to the door.

Karen: It will get better, Rooks.

Rooks (*groaning*): I hope so.

Karen: Bye, sweetie.

Her head still down, Rooks waives the mint and water.

Rooks: Bye.

***

SCENE 14 – Let Me Deal

Rooks is walking on her treadmill and eating an ice cream cone. On her TV she is playing Ever After. She is to the scene where Drew Barrymore is outside in the rain with her shoe. Her phone has been sitting on top the treadmill. Looking down, she notices she has a missed call. Licking the side of the cone, Rooks hits pause on the movie to listen to her message.

Rooks: I feel your pain, Drew.

Mom (*on voicemail*): Lovie, I got your message, and I know you're upset. I would be too. I imagine you've already transitioned into burn mode. Just don't overdo it, okay? Remember "Run." "Run" and "trust." The Lord must have other plans, so don't lose heart.

Somehow it will all be okay. And don't forget, carrots and Sundays clothes[43] can be comforting too. Love you. Talk to you later.

Totally oblivious to anything else around her, Rooks allows herself to move backward on the treadmill and fall into her cushy chair to finish her cone. Outside her window, her crush is arriving home. Looking up, he sees Rooks' transition and smiles.

***

SCENE 15 – I Hate to Move It, Move It[44]

It is official: Rooks has moved to the front of the office. Her client files sit in boxes around the desk. As she prepares to work, she notices dust, fingernail clippings, and something sticky around the computer. She finds a tissue and starts to clean.

Bruce (*coming down the hallway from his office*): Don't you just love this?

Rooks (*closing the tissue of fingernails in her hand*): It is *tremendous...*

Bruce: I think so too! I feel more and more positive about this *every* day, don't you? Change is such a good thing.

Rooks: It's the only thing that's constant. Hey, Bruce –

Bruce: And Lindsay is going to be phenomenal!

Rooks: Uh, Bruce, don't you think she's a tad... new... and somewhat inexperienced?

Bruce: Ah, but I've got a feeling.

Rooks: Like the flash mob at Oprah's opening[45]?

---

[43] At least that's what they advise in *Hello, Dolly*.
[44] Slight variation of Reel 2 Real's version.

Bruce: I don't know what that is. But you, you must be excited! This is a new adventure. You know, most people can only hope for such an opportunity.

Bruce starts to whistle as he walks down the hallway back to his office.

Rooks opens the tissue in her hand and looks at the fingernail clippings.

Rooks: Yes, this is quite the opportunity. Ugh.

She throws the clippings in the trash. She wipes down what she can, tries to settle in, and gets to work. She is putting a file on the shelf behind her when Lindsay enters the front door, her arms full of bags (of what looks like décor).

Lindsay (*cheerfully*): Good morning!

Rooks (*noticing the clock*): Good afternoon.

Lindsay: Oh, no, no, no. Did Bruce not tell you? We need you to keep your files in the other room. Otherwise, it will look too cluttered out here.

Rooks: Lindsay, I've got it mostly organized. I've just need to finish settling in.

Lindsay: No, we've got to look professional.

Rooks: And you think it won't? If I'm going to be up here, I need my files, else how am I supposed to work? X-ray vision? Telekinesis?

Lindsay: Why, one file at a time, silly.

Rooks: And when a client calls and needs an answer to a question right away?

Lindsay: Then you put them on hold and go get the file.

Rooks: The phone rings every 15 seconds. That means each time someone calls, I'll have to get up, walk down the hall, grab the file,

---

[45] Coolest. Flash. Mob. Ever. Courtesy of the Black-Eyed Peas and the city of Chicago.

come back down the hall, take them off hold, answer the question, and then put the file away.

Lindsay: That doesn't sound too complicated to me.

Rooks: By the time I get the file, the next person will be calling. I don't think it's realistic with the time lapse.

Lindsay: Then I guess you'll have to walk a little faster, won't you?

Rooks watches as Lindsay saunters down the hall and into Bruce's office.

Rooks *(under her breath):* She's haa-tched!

***

SCENE 16 – Watch Your Back, Bubba

With the onset of so many work frustrations, Rooks heads to the hospital to visit her mom.

Rooks: Hey, Mama. I figured you'd be here.

Mom: My home away from home.

Rooks *(waiving):* Hi, Edith.

Edith: Hi, sweetheart. Good to see you again.

Rooks: You too.

Mom: See you in a bit, Edith *(closing Edith's door).*

Rooks: How's she doing?

Mom: As good as can be expected. Keep her in your prayers, though, will you?

Rooks: You know I will.

Mom: And how are you? What news of Lindsay today? *(She puts her arm around Rooks' shoulder.)*

Rooks: Let's just say, Bruce Frankenstein[46] has outdone himself, and he doesn't even know it.

Mom: In other words, Lindsay is still taking advantage?

The two start walking toward the nurse's station.

Rooks: By coming in late everyday? Yes, yes, she is. And Graham is starting to follow suit. And here I was supposed to be training her. I can't train a person who isn't there.

Mom: And? What else? Vent on, my child.

Rooks: And the other day she asked me to help her with some case files –

Mom: - which you did –

Rooks: - which I did – because she claimed she was still trying to get her bearings – and when I went to return them, she was watching Netflix.[47]

Mom: Game of Thrones?[48]

Rita: The Sopranos?[49]

Rooks: 90210[50] – the new version.

Mom: A different kind of stabbing.

Rooks: Coupled with lessons on the latest fashion trends.

Rita: Ehn, give me Jason Priestley anyday.

Rooks: Don't I know it.

Mom: So did you say anything?

---

[46] Gotta love that Mary Shelley classic.
[47] What did we do before binge-watching for hours on end? *Is it dark outside? Do I need to go to work? Who cares? Let's watch another episode.*
[48] Recent, violent show where anyone can die.
[49] Fairly recent, violent show where anyone can die... by the mob.
[50] Fairly recent drama about California teens where anyone can die... just kidding.

Rooks: I was too shocked. Plus, I don't want to lose my job. Would you believe it? She now has the power to fire me.

Mom: Yeah, but that's not like you to keep silent.

Rooks: Well, it's different with you. I can tell you anything.

Mom: Lovie, you've got to learn to carry that over. It'll reduce your suffering. Just be tactful.

Rita: Mmm-hmmm.

Rooks: I don't know what to do. I've got to watch my tongue. But it definitely is hard. I've been working to make sure we're covered, but she's claiming "exhaustion" from all these supposed late hours.

Rita: "To get things done?"

Rooks (*nodding*): Yeah, except nothing changes. So, at first, I thought maybe she is trying to learn. Maybe she is The Apprentice.[51] But then I saw what's-his-face dance across her screen, and I knew better.

Rita: Rob Estes?

Rooks: It might have been.

Rita: I still prefer Jason.

Rooks: I know. Me too.

Mom: Sounds like you've got Scarlett[52] in your midst.

Rooks: Which means she's going to steal my man and drive Rhett away?

Mom: Not while I'm alive. But be careful, okay?

Rita: Never trust an unnatural blonde.

Rooks: Aren't you –

Rita: These are extensions.

---

[51] Another popular TV show, now hosted by The Terminator!?!
[52] Hard to believe, I know, but the book presents a more devious and manipulative character than the one portrayed by Vivian Leigh.

Mom: Try not to dwell on it – the situation, not the extensions.

Rita: Right. Go out. Be social.

Mom: And don't lose hope. Dream like Pippin[53]; climb like Maria[54]. I know it's an adjustment, but there's a purpose in it somewhere.

Rita: Feeling pumped?

Rooks (*laughing*): Yes! Yes, I am. Good pep talk.

Mom: Okay, then break!

***

SCENE 17 – Keeping the Neighborhood Watch

Rooks is on the way to her apartment when Elisa flags her down.

Elisa: Rooks! Woo-hoo! Rooks! (*running to catch up*) Hey, missy, are you alright? I've been chasing you from the corner.

Rooks: Oh, Elisa, I'm so sorry. I was lost in thought. It's been kind of day.

Elisa: I'm sorry to hear that! That's too bad. I bet the party will cheer you up, though! You're still planning to come, right?

Rooks: To the party? Oh, no, that's this week, isn't it?

Elisa: It's tomorrow.

Rooks: Tomorrow? Oh my goodness.

Elisa: Don't worry. You needn't feel obligated. It'll be okay.

Rooks: No, no, no. I told you I would come, and I will. I'm just tired, that's all. I should be fine by then.

Elisa: Are you sure?

---

[53] Stellar play about a guy who dreams...
[54] Those Von Trapps had to have been in excellent health.

Rooks: I'm sure. Trust me.

Elisa (*getting excited*): Oh, goodie! Because I have someone I would love for you to meet! I know you hate set-ups, but this guy is super nice. In fact, you may have already seen him. He's new to the apartment. Now, he just recently got out of a serious relationship, but don't let that scare you. They were together three years – major intense. He and my fiancé have known each other for years, and I think you two would really hit it off.

Rooks (*reluctantly*): Oh, okay. Sure. That sounds great. I'll give him a try.

Elisa: Really? That is so fantastic. Oh my goodness. This is going to be a-maz-ing! And when you're married and having your first child, you can name her after me!

***

SCENE 18 – The World of Trivia (And Trivial) Get-togethers

There are about six to eight people in Elisa's apartment. They are seated about on the couch and chairs, and Elisa is ready to get started.

Elisa (*squealing*): I'm excited you're all here! Thank you so much for coming. And just think, if it's this much fun now, then it's going to be spectacular at the wedding! Only a few more weeks!

Roger: Take a breath, hon.

Elisa: I know, I know (*giving him a peck*). Okay, so let's start with a game. Who doesn't like trivia? We'll break into teams. You guys will be yellow (*motioning to half*), and you'll be orange. Oh! And I almost forgot! Would anyone like something to drink? Of course, there's water, but we've also got lemonade and orange soda! Roger would be happy to bring you what you like.

Roger: I would. Indeed.

Roger gets everyone's order before heading to the kitchen. Close to Rooks, there sits a boy and girl.

Andy: I'm Andy, by the way.

Rooks: Nice to meet you. Rooks. (*They shake hands.*)

Andy: Rooks, as in …?

Rooks: Multiple chess pieces? Yes, my dad has a serious obsession.

Andy: Is that right?

Rooks: It is. I consider myself lucky, though.

Andy: Huh?

Rooks: Because Slugger was the other option.

Andy: Oh.

Rooks: He also loves baseball.

Andy (*making a face*): How interesting.

Carie (*under her breath*): More like weird.

Rooks: Excuse me?

Carie (*with a fake voice*): How fascinating. I'm Carie.

Rooks: Like the movie[55]?

Carie: But with one 'r.'

Andy: Which means she's only ½ evil.

Carie: Oh, you. (*They both cackle.*)

Rooks: I see. (*Roger hands her a glass of water, and she takes a drink.*) Thank you. I take it you've known each other for a while?

Andy: Carie and I go way back.

---

[55] Let this be a lesson to all: Nothing good ever comes from pig's blood.

Carie (*touching his knee*): Way, way back.

Andy: We're friends of Elisa. And you? (*condescendingly*) Why are you here?

Rooks: I live in the apartment upstairs, across the way.

Carie: How quaint.

Andy: So then you know Elisa?

Rooks: Yes, I do. We're friends.

Andy: Is that right?

Elisa (*at the front of the room*): Does everyone have a drink? Shall we begin?

There are nods and yeses from everyone.

Elisa: Oh, goodie! Then it's time. Yellow team, we will start with you. Are you ready?

Andy: We are.

Elisa: Alright, alright, alright.[56] First trivia question. We'll go super easy to begin. (*drawing a card from a box*) How delightful! It's from literature. Ready? "Who wrote *Alice in Wonderland*?"

Andy (*without hesitation*): Lewis Carroll.

Elisa: Very good, Andy-man.

Carie (*stroking his arm*): You're so smart, Andy.

Andy: Give me a tough one, Lise.

Elisa: Okay, Mr. Smartypants. (*drawing another question*) We've got a harder question coming your way. Same category. Here we go. You ready? (*They nod.*) "Which is Shakespeare's bloodiest play?"

Andy hesitates.

Rooks (*to her teammates*): *Titus Andronicus.*

---

[56] Said more like Outkast than Matthew McConaughey.

Andy: Are you sure? Noooo, that can't be it.

Carie: Yeah. I would have definitely remembered that.

Rooks: Because...

Carie: Because I went to a prestigious university, *and* I took a Shakespeare class.

Rooks: Oh. Okay. So then what would you suggest (*drinking more of her water*)?

Carie: I would say *Hamlet*. So many people die in that one. Or what's that one with that really proud Roman guy?

Rooks: *Julius Caesar*? *Coriolanus*?

Carie (*to Andy*): Yeah. Doesn't he kill a lot of people?

Rooks downs more of her water.

Elisa: I need an answer.

Andy: *Hamlet* sounds good to me. You've always been the brainy type.

Carie: Oh, Andy! Thank you.

Elisa: The timer is winding down.... Come on, team! Your response?

Carie and Andy: *Hamlet*.

Elisa: Is that your final answer?[57] (*They both nod.*) Oh, I am so, so sorry! That is incorrect! Orange team, do you have a guess?

Steve (*breaking from the other group's huddle*): *Titus Andronicus*?

Elisa: That is correct!

Carie: I can't believe I missed that.

Andy (*to Rooks*): How could you have possibly known that?

Carie: Let me guess. Your dad is a literature fanatic?

Rooks: No. That would be my mom – former English major.

Andy (*rolling his eyes*): Right.

---

[57] The phrase made popular by the one-and-only Regis Philman.

Andy and Carie exchange looks and then turn away to talk to each other. As the game continues, the cute neighbor enters the apartment. He makes the rounds, giving all the girls (except Rooks) a hug and shaking hands with the guys. He introduces himself to Andy. When he gets to Rooks, he gives her a nod, and then goes to sit with the other team. Rooks looks over to see Elisa pointing and mouthing "That's the guy."

Elisa: Welcome, Christian. I'm glad you could make it! Now, yellow team, we are back to you. I hope you've got your singing caps on because we are on to musicals!

Andy: I don't suppose you know much about that, do you?

Rooks (*drinking, swishing, and swallowing the last remains of her cup*): Mmm. Will you excuse me a moment? Refill.

Rooks takes her glass, goes into the kitchen, and sets it on the counter. For a moment, she stops. Then, eyeing the fridge, she walks over and opens the door. Searching the shelves, she comes across a tub of cool whip. She takes it out and opens the lid.

Rooks: Such a lovely smell.

She sets the cool whip and lid on the counter and begins to search through the drawers.

Rooks: What? Nobody carries ladles anymore?

Finally, in one drawer, she finds a large spoon.

Rooks: Perfect.

Game face on, she returns to the cool whip and is about to thrust in her spoon, when the handsome guy enters the kitchen.

Christian: Hey.

Rooks (*with a classic caught-in-the-act face*): Oh, hi. Hello. How's it going? (*She is holding the spoon straight up into the air.*)

Christian: Good. Good. And you?

Rooks: Not too shabby. Just thought I'd, uh, you know, get a jumpstart on dessert.

Christian: I can see that. The name's Christian.

Rooks: Rooks (*extending the spoon to shake, then realizing her error*).

Christian: Not a big trivia fan, I take it?

Rooks: Uh… no, it's not that. Um, it's… pure sugar motivation, that's all.

Christian: Hmmm. Well, then who I am to stop you?

He steps closely toward her, reaches behind her back to the cool whip, and takes a swipe of it with his finger.

Christian (*putting the cool whip into his mouth*): Great idea.

He walks out, leaving her speechless. Once Rooks has recomposed, she puts away the cool whip and goes back into the other room to the party. She notices her team has repositioned themselves so as to block her from rejoining the group, so instead of staying, she quietly slips out the door.

***

SCENE 19 – And now we GNO

Rooks, and her gal pals Harper, Denise, and Marley, indulge in some cheesecake at Food Therapy.

Harper: Wow, that is amazing! Talk about a turn-on!

Rooks: Initiative is sexy.

Marley: As is cheesecake.

All together: Mmm-hmmm.

Harper: Men just don't realize.

Denise: What makes it so hard, I wonder? To where they always need a directive?

Marley: I blame El Niño.

Rooks: Beats me. It's like mom always says, if it were up to Adam, he would have been like, "Hey, Eve. You're pretty cool. We should hang out sometime."

All together: Mmm-hmmm.

Denise: Glad Christian is different.

Harper: Yeah, but is he really ready to date though? To commit to another person?

Rooks: It seemed like he was fine. It didn't appear like he had any baggage. Maybe it was a pleasant separation?

All together: Mmmmm.

Harper: Is there such a thing?

Marley: I've never heard of it.

Denise: In any case, serious relationship aside – we're glad he stepped up. But the others... they sound lame.

Harper: Yeah. What was their deal anyway?

Rooks: I don't know, but it was horrible. I was ready to call and have you sing "Soft Kitty[58]" to me.

Harper: Ugh. Elitism. I will never understand it – or affluenza,[59] for that matter.

Marley: Me either.

---

[58] What Sheldon has Penny do on *The Big Bang Theory* when he needs comfort.

[59] The so-called condition that renders the wealthy irresponsible... and stupid.

Harper: You would think with Elisa being so nice, that her friends would be too.

Rooks: I guess you never know with single-tons. Sometimes outsiders aren't welcome.

Harper: Did you say anything?

Rooks: No, I let it pass.

Harper: Rooks! For the love, speak your mind!

Rooks: I do!

Harper: Outside of your mother.

Rooks: I do!

Harper: And your father. You are not a doormat.

Denise: So do you think he knew?

Rooks (*playfully*): My father? No, I don't think so.

Denise: No, Christian. Did Elisa say anything to him about setting the two of you up?

Rooks: I have no idea.

Marley: I bet he knew. They always know. Then they just toy with your emotions.

Harper: Except for Phil.

Marley: Except for Phil.

They all sigh.

Denise: So maybe that's why he went into the kitchen? Not to toy but to follow you.

Marley: Yes, let's analyze.

Rooks: Or maybe he was sleepwalking? I don't know.

Harper: Tell me, what do you know? Anything?

Rooks: I know he was really sexy... (*collapsing over onto the table*)

Harper: There you go, girl (*patting her back*). Admission is the first step.[60]

Denise: And have you seen him since?

Rooks (*still bent over on the table*): We had a small interchange in the parking lot.

Harper: Was it more than just "hi?"

Rooks (*muffled*): He asked me about my day.

Harper: Great. So we got a "How are you?" That's progress.

Michael comes over to refill glasses and hears the last bit of the girls' conversation.

Michael: Found the man of your dreams, did you?

Rooks (*sitting up, blushing*): No. Maybe. I don –

Harper: She doesn't know.

Rooks (*still red*): It's just nice to have someone to like, you know what I mean?

Michael: I think I do. (*He smiles, and then walks away*).

Denise (*watching Michael*): I think he –you know what? Never mind. Let's finish this, shall we?

The girls dive into the rest of the cheesecake. Denise stares at Michael, who turns to look back at her.

***

SCENE 20 – Here Comes the Storm… do do do do

At the office, everything is in chaos. The phones are ringing off the hook, the fax is beeping, and emails keep popping up on Rooks'

---

[60] Sometimes easier said than done.

computer. She's got the copiers and printers going in the next office.
There are files stacked on her desk and nearby on the floor. Two
businessmen are there in reception waiting for their appointment, and
Rooks is the only person in the office.

Bruce (*entering*): Good morning! How are things going this morning?

Rooks (*covering the receiver with her hand*): They're alright.

(*Motioning to the people in the area in front of her*) Your 10 o'clock is ready.

Bruce (*turning around*): Wonderful! How nice to meet you! (*He shakes their hands*). Follow me, please.

The men get up to follow Bruce to the Conference room.

Rooks (*into the phone*): Yes, sir. I understand. We will have your order ready by this afternoon. I am working on your flier as we speak. Yes, sir. I will send you the tracking number…. The business cards are done. (*She hangs up the phone and goes to her email.*)

Bruce (*coming back up*): I need their information. Do you have their file?

Rooks: Lindsay has it.

Bruce: Great! I'll go get it from her. (*He starts down the hallway.*)

Rooks (*calling after him without stopping her work*): She's not here.

Bruce (*coming back up*): She's not here? Hmm. She probably had something to do. Nevermind, I'll just have Graham help me find it. (*He starts back down the hallway*).

Rooks (*calling after him*): He's not here either.

Bruce (*coming back up*): He's not here either? Is he sick?

Rooks: I don't know. I haven't heard from him. They are both MIA.

Bruce: Well, do you think you can help me? (*The phone rings*.) When you're finished?

Rooks (*picking up the phone*): Sure. Bruce Levine's Advertizing Haven.

***

SCENE 21 – Lucy, I'm here!

An hour has passed, and things have calmed down somewhat at the office. Rooks has a file in front of her and is feverishly working to finish the client's request. Bruce has finished his appointment and is showing the men to the exit. As he starts back to his office, Lindsay and Graham enter.

Bruce (*turning around, arms wide*): Good morning, you two! So nice to see you.

Lindsay gives him a hug.

Bruce: Where have you been?

Lindsay: Graham and I were having breakfast.

Bruce: What a great idea! That's a tremendous way to build team unity.

Lindsay: I knew you'd like it.

Bruce: Next time we should all do lunch.

Graham: Yeah, totally, but then who would man the phones?

Lindsay: I'm sure Rooks could handle it.

Rooks looks stunned at the interchange; the others head to the back. The phone begins to ring, but Rooks is so lost she doesn't pick up right away. Lindsay appears at her desk.

Lindsay: You going to get that?

Rooks (*coming to*): What?

Lindsay: The phone. The phone is ringing. You know I can't answer.

Rooks (*picking it up*): Hello, Bruce Levine's Advertizing Haven. Hello? There's nobody there.

Lindsay: Well, of course not. You took too long.

Rooks: To say BLAH[61]? My bad.

Lindsay: You know when I was doing this, I never had these issues.

Rooks (*Taking a breath*): How can I help you, Lindsay?

Lindsay: I need to run an errand.

Rooks: Now? You just got here.

Lindsay: I need to go out. Do you have a problem with that?

Rooks (*holding back*): No. No more than usual.

Lindsay: Good. Because I want you to do me a favor.

Rooks: What's that?

Lindsay: I've got a client who keeps bothering me about something or another, and I need you to make him go away.

Rooks: You want me to kill him off?

Lindsay: No, I want –

Rooks: Do you have a preferred method?

Lindsay: Rooks! I want you to go through my email and respond to his and all the other client messages. You think you can handle that?

Rooks: Sure. I'll add it to my list.

Lindsay: Put it at the top. Oh, and do it out here. I don't want you in my office. I'll have Graham forward everything to you.

Rooks: Lindsay, you do realize I've got other clients I'm assisting (*motioning to the piles on her desk and toward the back office*).

---

[61] A wonderful acronym, fitting to most office jobs... unfortunately.

Lindsay: I don't care. This guy is annoying me, so do whatever, but get it done.[62]

Rooks: Fine. And when will you be back?

Lindsay: I don't know. I'm tired and my head hurts. Probably tomorrow.

Finished with her part of the conversation, Lindsay walks away. Two minutes later, with her purse in hand, Lindsay walks out the door.

***

SCENE 22 – I Heart Nice Gestures

Exhausted, Rooks arrives at her apartment to find a can of Reddi-wip on her doorstep with a bright red bow wrapped around it. Dropping her purse to the concrete, she kneels down to pick up the can, finding a note that reads "Utensils not required." A smile spreads across her face. She shakes the can, breaks open the seal, and sprays some of its contents into her mouth.

***

SCENE 23 – Whip while you Walk

On her treadmill, Rooks is at a slow jog while she talks to her mother about all that has transpired. On one side of the equipment is the Reddi-wip, and on the other, a bottle of water. As she fills her mother in, she sprays the delicious goodness into her mouth intermittently.

---

[62] Or as we like to say in the South, *Git er done.*

Rooks (*coming to a power walk*): Can I ask you a question?

Mom: Of course you can, lovie. Was that it?

Rooks: Not quite! Here goes: Would you still love me if I turned psychopath?

Granny (*in the background*): Don't count on it!

Mom: I think what she means to say is, "We'll consider it."

Granny (*in the background*): No, I don't.

Mom: Mom!

Rooks: I'm just not sure how much more of this I can take. It's like she's out to get me.

Mom: Well, she probably is. As Edith said, at the end of the day, she knows you should've gotten the job, so she has to defend her territory.

Rooks: A poor excuse. She's not a Chihuahua.

Mom: Have you talked to Bruce?

Rooks: No, it's fine. I can handle it.

Mom: There are other jobs out there.

Rooks: Yeah, but then I would have to start over, and I'm behind as it is.

Mom: Rooks –

Rooks: Ugh. Let's not talk about it anymore. Tell me about Edith! Is she doing better? Is the treatment working?

Mom: It's taking its toll, that's for sure. But she's a trooper. Tough as nails, that woman. And her son is such a sweetie. He comes by whenever he can.

Rooks: Mom –

Mom: Sorry. I know.

Rooks: I'll try to stop by as soon as I can.

Mom: Sounds like an excellent idea. She would like that. In the meantime, since you're wanting to stay, might I suggest you do squats or something when you're at your desk? Maybe that will help you keep cool – at least to a certain extent? Because try as I may, I don't know that I could justify "insanity" to the court.

Rooks (*spraying a huge blob into her mouth*): I'll do what I can.

***

SCENE 24 – Clouseau[63] Would Get It!

Close to the end of another work day, Rooks has a realization. She goes to Bruce's office to ask him about it.

Bruce: Come in.

Rooks: Hey, Bruce. I need to know what you want me to do. Lindsay left a little early again today, and she, uh, well, she forgot to give me my paycheck.

Bruce: Oh, surely not! I bet it's in on her desk.

Rooks: Um... okay.

Bruce: With all that she's got to do, she probably just forgot to hand it to you on her way out.

Rooks (*biting her tongue*): I understand. So what do you want me to do?

Bruce: Check her office first.

Rooks: And if it's not there?

---

[63] Vivez Peter Sellers! Comment il était le meilleur!

Bruce: Hmmm... if it's not there, then we have a problem, and I won't know what to do. That was always Karen's expertise.

Rooks: Sure, sure. Actually, Bruce, I do know how to print checks. I would just need the new password to access funds.

Bruce: Really? Why, that's tremendous. It shouldn't be too hard then. Maybe ask Graham? See if he knows it?

Rooks: Sure. I'll *check* it out.

***

SCENE 25 – Maybe Allen Luden[64] knows...

Rooks goes to Graham's office to see if he has the password.

Rooks: Graham?

Graham (*looking up from his computer, where he is watching a sports replay*): Dude, did you see the game?

Rooks: The game?

Graham: Yeah, the football game?

Rooks: Which one?

Graham (*opening a clip*): This one. Check it out, dude! A 1980's classic.

Rooks (*wincing*): Man, that is fierce. Too much for this 12th man.[65] So, question for you?

Graham: Sure. Whatcha need?

Rooks: I was wondering if you had Lindsay's password, in case I need to print off my check?

---

[64] Do you know the password?
[65] For the few... the proud... the dedicated fans.

Graham: You didn't get paid?

Rooks: You did?

Graham: Yeah, totally. She gave me my check yesterday.

Rooks: You're not serious.

Graham: I so am. I deposited it on the way in this morning – that's why I was late. Well, that and I had to catch up on some recaps.

Rooks: So maybe mine is in her office?

Graham: That would be my guess.

***

SCENE 26 – Inside the Devil's Lair

Rooks goes to Lindsay's office to look around. She notices the new curtains and the plushy chair behind the desk. The bulletin board looks like a page out of a teeny-bopper magazine. She sits down at Lindsay's desk to sort through everything to find her check. There are magazines, nail polish, and a couple of nail files, amongst other things. It seems the only thing missing is the fertility goddess[66]. At one point during her search, she mutters, "Good grief. Should I worry about a glitter explosion?" Hope as she may, Rooks' check is not there.

***

SCENE 27 – Back to Bruce Street

Once again, Rooks knocks on Bruce's door to see what he wants her to do about this situation.

---

[66] Think Doris Day in *Pillow Talk*.

Bruce: Come in.

Rooks: Bruce, I have searched through every perfume ad and cut out, and it's not there. My check is nowhere to be found, and Graham doesn't know the password.

Bruce: Hmmm… I'll bet she'll be back later to take care of it.

Rooks: Does she have supernatural powers? Because I leave in twenty. And Graham has his check. She gave it to him yesterday.

Bruce: Hmph. Really? That's interesting. Well, do you think you could wait until Monday?

Rooks: To come back to work?

Bruce: To get your check?

Rooks: Well, I was hoping to eat. And maybe pay a few bills. It's kind of a thing.

Bruce: The way I see it, I don't think we have any other options.

Rooks (*getting an idea*): Wait a second. Maybe we do.

***

SCENE 28 – Holla at Your Girl

Rooks goes to the front of the office to get her purse. Inside, she finds her phone and scrolls down her contact list until she reaches Karen's number.

Karen: Why, hello, my child with a different mother. How are you?

Rooks: Swell, just swell. The Apocalypse[67] is near, in case you didn't know.

Karen: That bad, huh?

Rooks: How could you tell?

Karen: Because you sound... beaten. And a little worn.

Rooks: Let's just say I've seen better days.[68]

Karen: Sublime. Have you said anything to Bruce?

Rooks: No, because Bruce is as Bruce does. He wouldn't know how to buttle.[69]

Karen: You really think he'd let Lindsay fire you?

Rooks: I think he'd let Lindsay enter North Korea if that's what she wanted.

Karen: Hmmm. How comforting.

Rooks: Isn't that the truth? Anyways, I need your help. Lindsay "forgot" to pay me before she left today.

Karen: Ouch. It's one thing to forget your slip, but another to forget a girl's paycheck. That gets into Federal law.

Rooks: Yeah. Don't I know it.

Karen: So what do you need me for? I showed you how to do paychecks. Don't tell me you've forgotten!

Rooks: No, I haven't forgotten. Apparently, Lindsay changed the password.

Karen: That evil nymph! Well, good thing there's an override.

Rooks: I was hoping you would say that.

Karen: Head to the back. I'll walk you through it.

---

[67] EKE! Make sure you're ready!

[68] A great song by...

[69] In other words, he hasn't a *Clue*.

Rooks returns to Lindsay's office, and with Karen's help, she is able to print out her paycheck.

***

SCENE 29 – On to better things

With her paycheck in tow, Rooks goes home to her apartment feeling victorious. She runs into Christian, who is dressed and ready to go jogging.

Christian: Perfect timing. Care to join me?

Rooks: Sure. But I would need to change.

Christian: That's alright. I can wait.

Rooks: Okay... but you do realize I'm not that great of a jogger, right?

Christian: Oh, come on. I've seen you.

Rooks: And you were impressed? I am such a pseudo-jogger. A poser, if you will.

Christian: It looked good to me. What do you say?

Rooks: Um... yeah. Let's do it. Then I can maintain my daily sugar consumption, and it'll kill the stress. Work is a little – (*She makes a hand motion.*)

Christian: Fair enough. Let's see how it goes, then.

Rooks: Alright. Okay. I'll get changed.

Rooks enters her apartment and does the Guinness World Record change into her workout apparel: a pair of yoga pants, a shirt from 1996, and Christmas socks. When she comes out, Christian is stretching.

Christian: Pretty cute. Shall we?

Rooks: Let's do this.

And they're off in a flirty, but productive jog. Upon her return, Rooks falls onto her bed completely happy. She picks up her phone to text her mom and gal pals: "Best jog ever!"

***

SCENE 30 – Searching for Strategy

Rooks has stopped by the hospital to check on her mom and Edith.

Mom: Remind me to send Karen aromatherapy or something. The nerve of that girl.

Edith: I recommend lavender.

Rooks: She claims she has 28 days to pay me.

Edith: What did your offer letter say?

Mom: Listen to Edith. She's former HR.

Rooks: Bi-weekly.

Edith: Then you need to bring it up with that boss of yours. Love these cookies, by the way. Mmmm. Remind me of home.

Rooks: You are welcome. I definitely did not make them.

Mom: But she knows where to get them.

Edith: Well, they are delicious. And far better than some of the stuff I get around here.[70]

Mom: I see nothing. I know nothing.

Rooks: Anyways, I would talk to Bruce, but you know he's not going to listen. It's like he's on another planet or something.

---

[70] The transition to institutionalized food can be a difficult one... Bless those that cook and those that must eat...

Mom: Mars?

Rooks: Neptune.

Edith: You need a stronger voice.

Mom: That's what I said.

Rooks: And here I thought the parrot was dead.[71] Tell you what. This Friday I'll try switching places with Adele.[72]

Mom: Freakier things have happened.[73]

Rooks: So true. But this feels like a losing battle, like I'm waging war against Supergirl.

Edith: Only she's not that super. She's like one of those rich girls Hall & Oates[74] sing about.

Mom: Or Goliath – who was defeated, need I remind you.

Rooks: Okay, so then what do I do? How do I get stone to forehead?[75] Because this is getting to the point of unbearable.

Edith: After almost missing a paycheck, I would think you would have passed that point already.

Mom: She's pretty patient, Edith, with the self-discipline of a nun.

Edith: A little too patient, if you ask me. I'd take a shot at aggression, if I were you.

Rooks: How? What do I do?

Mom and Edith look at each other and then at Rooks.

Mom: That's a good question, lovie. But you're going to have to run those buns and come up with your own solution. And I – or rather, we – will support you in whatever you choose.

---

[71] Monty Python, anyone? *This parrot is no more! He has ceased to be!*
[72] Hello?!? It's Adele, the modern-day singer with an amazing voice.
[73] Like parents and children switching bodies...
[74] About a girl? Or about a BOY? Ooh. Intrigue.
[75] The method by which David killed Goliath.

Edith: Absolutely.

***

SCENE 31 – Psst! Where've you been?

Rooks, a bit tired from another long work day, is on her way back to her apartment.

Elisa: Rooks! You are a difficult girl to track down, missy!

Rooks: Oh, I'm sorry, Elisa. Work has been quite the beast. I've had to stay late everyday this past week.

Elisa: No worries. I'm just long overdue in giving you this (*handing her a thank you card*). Now I know I could have left it on your door step long ago, but some things are better in person, don't you think? Anyways, thank you for coming to the party. It was simply perfect having you there!

Rooks: Thank you for the thank you, Elisa. But really, it was nice of you to invite me.

Elisa: Of course! That's what neighbor's do. And did you get a chance to meet Christian?

Rooks: I did. We had a run-in in the kitchen.

Elisa: And? What did you think?

Rooks: He's nice. In fact, we went jogging the other week.

Elisa: What? You did? Oh my goodness! That is amazing! So, you're really hitting it off? Just wait 'til I tell Roger! I am convinced you two would make the perfect couple.

Rooks: I guess we'll see... So, you ready for the big day?

Elisa: Oh my goodness! Let me just say, I am so excited! You're going to be there, right?

Rooks: I wouldn't miss it for the world.

***

SCENE 32 – Here Comes the Bride

Rooks gets ready for Elisa and Roger's wedding, putting on an elegant, but simple, form-fitting dress. On her way out, she runs into Christian, who is dressed in a tuxedo.

Christian: Heading my way?

Rooks (*finding the words*): Wow... Yes... I believe I am.

Christian: Well, then, shall we?

Rooks gets into Christian's car and together they ride to the ceremony. They watch the sweet exchange of vows by the happy couple. Later, after Christian has greeted all the men and hugged all the ladies, the two share a few meaningful moments dancing under the glow of the Chinese lanterns at the reception. Andy and Carie look on with disdain. When it is time to return to the apartment, Christian walks Rooks up the stairs and to her door.

Rooks: Thank you for a wonderful evening. Honestly, with work being so cray-cray as of late, this was nice.

Christian: I'm glad I could help. And maybe, if you want, I could help take your mind off of those other things (*He puts his arm on the door frame and leans in toward her.*[76]) You think you'd like to –

---

[76] As in "Hey, Luce. Is this guy bothering you... cause it looks like he's leaning."

His phone rings, interrupting him and his leaning, thwarting what would have been a good night kiss.

Rooks: I guess it is all in the timing.[77]

Christian: I'm sorry. I should probably take this. Will you excuse me?

Rooks: Sure.

As he walks down the stairs, she can hear him answer, "Yes, this is he. How may I help you? Yes, of course I remember you... You want me to what? Oh, sure, that's fine. When would you like me to meet her?"

***

SCENE 33 – Tick, Tock, Tick, Tock

Rooks had gone into Lindsay's office to grab a file and is heading back down the hall to her desk when Lindsay enters the front door.

Lindsay: Have you been in my office?

Rooks: Yes, the client called and said he wanted his brochures today.

Lindsay: You shouldn't have gone in my office.

Rooks: I needed his file so I could review his order.

Lindsay: Unacceptable. That is my space. You cannot invade my sanctuary.

Rooks (*struggling to holding back*): So suddenly we're in France? This is an office, Lindsay, and I was doing work, not invading the church.[78]

Lindsay: I don't care. I'm the Office Manager. Don't let me catch you in there again, or there will be consequences.

Rooks: What does that mean?

---

[77] So says David Ives.
[78] Sanctuary! Sanctuary!

Lindsay: You know what it means.

Lindsay storms down the hall, and Rooks mutters under her breath,
"Good grief. Well, at least there's Christian."

***

SCENE 34 – Here You Come Again[79]

Rooks is happy to see Christian again as she gets home. She lights up
as she puts her car in park. As they near each other, she notices he is
dressed nicely and has a small gift in his hand. When he sees her, he
starts acting strange.

Rooks: Hey! Long time no see.

Christian: Hi.

Rooks: You look good.

Christian: Um, thank you.

Rooks: On your way out?

Christian: Yeah. I am actually. (*Pause*) Listen, I don't really have time
to talk right now.

Rooks: Oh. Late for an important date?[80]

Christian (*looking guilty*): Something like that.

Rooks: Well, do you want to come over later? Maybe watch a movie
or a workout video or something?

Christian: I can't.

Rooks: Oh, okay. Then perhaps we could try for something this
weekend?

---

[79] A reference for classic country lovers.
[80] The White Rabbit would understand.

Christian: I'm sorry, Rooks, but I've really got to go.

He walks on and gets into his car without looking back.

Rooks (*watching him leave*): What just happened?

***

SCENE 35 – Soul Therapy

Crestfallen, Rooks sits at a table at Food Therapy, stirring her water and gazing out the window.

Michael: Want your usual?

Rooks holds up her glass.

Michael: I mean the rest of it?

Rooks: No, I'm alright. This is fine.

Michael: Seriously? You don't want any cheesecake? Was there a shift in the time space continuum?

Rooks: Worse – a reverse shift.

Michael: Uh-oh. What's wrong?

Rooks: I think I just got the brush-off.

Michael: From the love of your life?

Rooks: Well, no, but from someone I thought had potential. Amazing potential.

Michael: Oh, I see.

Rooks: I don't even know what I did – if I did anything. It all felt so magical – like we had this connection and everything was falling into place. I was thinking maybe "final rose?"[81]

---

[81] Oh, *The Bachelor*. Enough said.

Michael (*clearing his throat*): And I take it work hasn't gotten any better?

Rooks: You're two for two. It's like, subconsciously, I know the horse is dead, but I can't bring myself to put down the stick.

Michael: That poor animal. I'm sorry, Rooks.

Rooks: It's alright. It's not your fault. I'm in a race against myself.

Michael: I understand that one.

Rooks: Let me ask you this. Does it ever seem like no matter how hard you try, you're not going to get there?

Michael: Get where?

Rooks: To love? To success? To having it all?

Michael: I'm a 32-year-old waiter. There may have been a few curveballs.

Rooks: Right. Point taken. But isn't it supposed to? At some point, isn't it all supposed to come together?

Michael: Life? Only if it's the board game. There you get paid to have children.

Rooks: But what about hard work? Shouldn't that ensure you get somewhere?

Michael: Of course it does, but that doesn't mean it happens overnight.

Rooks: And why did I bother to get an education? My degree is worthless. If you want a job, you have to have experience. But if you have experience and don't have an education, you can't get hired either. So then you end up at a job that kind of coincides with what you want to do, only it's not what you really want to do. Oh, why do I even care? None of this – none of it matters.

He sits down across from her.

Michael: It matters. Hey, look at me. It matters.

Rooks: I would love to believe you. But honestly, it feels like Justice for All but me. The bad guy wins again.

Michael: Is that your new motto? Rooks, seriously, you have got to cheer up. This isn't you. You have so much going on for you. You have a job. You have great friends. You've got me, and I've got cheesecake. (*She looks up at him.*) How's your family?

Rooks (*muttering*): They're pretty awesome.

Michael: So then you've got them too. Rooks, life and happiness are about looking at what you do have, not at what you don't. You know what someone told me recently?

Rooks: What?

Michael: There comes a time when you have to trust God.

Rooks: Oh, good gracious. Yes, I know. My mother tells me the same thing all the time – in oh-so-many-words.

Michael: Well, she has a point.

Rooks: Maybe… But goodness, it's so frustrating!

Michael: I know it is! Believe me, I get it. I wear an apron for a living. I pour water. Trust me, I have been schooled in the University of Life's Challenges. But let me just say this: It's going to be okay. Things will work out.

Rooks: How utterly cliché.

Michael: Hey, don't discount my words of wisdom! For all you know, I could be a modern-day Socrates.

Rooks (*lighting a little*): Fine, fine, Yoda. I suppose. Tell me this then, oh wise one: Will I have a geriatric pregnancy?

Michael (*laughing*): Only if you want to. Although my medical expertise is limited, I think you're going to be fine – just fine. Now (*standing up*) can I get you something? At least bring you a lemon?

Rooks: Sure. Great. Shall we make lemonade?

***

SCENE 36 – That's What Friends are For

Rooks is on the phone with Harper trying to figure out what is happening.

Rooks: No, I haven't seen him. It's like he's disappeared. "Where did Christian go? I don't know. He's vanished." How is that even possible?

Harper: I don't know, girl, but it seems a bit suspicious, if you ask me.

Rooks: Maybe he's got a crazy work scene? He told me he was a banker – one of the head ones.

Harper: Do bankers keep late hours?

Rooks: They did in *Mary Poppins*.

Harper: Mmmmm, so maybe... Or maybe he's...

Rooks: No, don't say it! Don't go all Behrendt[82] on me. It was going so well.

Harper: Then give him a little more time. But not too much, okay? If he doesn't appear like a scene out of Sixteen Candles,[83] then you need

---

[82] True as it may be, does any girl ever want to hear *He's Just Not That Into You*? I don't think so.

[83] Ah, 80s classics. Bless you, Molly Ringwald.

to move on. You're 34. This is not the time to let infatuation walk all over you.

***

SCENE 37– Oh No She Didn't

It is close to closing time at the office. Rooks is finishing up her work, when Christian walks through the door with some flowers.

Rooks: Welcome to Bruce Levine's Adv – (*looking up*) Hi. What are you doing here?

Christian (*completely thrown*): I. I, uh –

Rooks: Did Elisa tell you I work here?

Christian: No. She didn't.

Rooks: So then what are you doing here? How did you find me?

Christian (*looking embarrassed*): Actually, I'm not here for you. I'm here for –

Rooks: You're here for –

Lindsay (*coming down the hall*): Is that my guy? Oh, it is! (*giving him a kiss*) Give me a second. I need to get my purse.

Rooks (*before Lindsay can leave*): I'm sorry. You two know each other? H-h-how do you know each other?

Lindsay: My brother Andy met him at some party a while back. Then he saw him again at this wedding and thought we should hook up.

Rooks: Your brother?

Lindsay: Andy. Yes, he is the best. He called to set us up, and now here we are. I'll get my purse.

Christian: Rooks. Rooks. I –

Rooks (*starting to find her voice*): - am not interested. What you mean to say is you're not interested.

Christian: I'm sorry.

Rooks: No, no. Don't worry about it. I get it. This was just some sort of Steve Harvey gaffe.[84]

Christian: Rooks.

Rooks (*her voice getting stronger*): It was my mistake. All mine. But can I ask you something, though? Because here I thought we were starting something. Did I do something to dissuade you? You know, like trash talk your mother?

Christian: No, you didn't.

Rooks: Murder your brother?

Christian: I don't have a brother.

Rooks: Well, not anymore.

Christian: Rooks!

Rooks: I just want to understand. This makes no sense to me.

Lindsay (*returning, having overheard everything*): He's not interested in you, okay? And why would he be? You're just a secretary.

***

SCENE 38 – Moving Past Madness

Rooks is at the kitchen table at her parent's house, fiddling with the chess pieces. Her dad sits across from her while her mother is finishing dishes.

---

[84] Awkward...so sorry Colombia.

Rooks: Is it always going to be like this?

Mom: Lovie. How many times have I told you? That is the curse of being pretty.

Rooks: Yes, yes, I know. Only Jennifer Aniston[85] understands my pain.

Dad: So you struck out. You start another game. You move forward, you move back.[86] You don't let it bench you.

Mom (*drying her hands and handing her a cookie*): What your dad means to say is, "Don't dwell on it." I mean, what he did was wrong, but at least it didn't get as far as Willoughby.[87]

Dad (*motioning for Rooks to give him the cookie*): Precisely. "Remember Morgenstern. You'll be a lot happier."[88]

Rooks (*taking a bite of the cookie and passing the rest of it to her father*): Wow. Thanks for the sympathy?

Dad: Your mother and I did not raise you to be someone who wallows.[89]

Granny (*in the background*): Neither did I!

Mom: Thanks, mom! (*to Dad*) Insulin.

Dad (*taking a bite*): Done. So now, now can I set you up? Please?

Rooks: I don't know, Dad. Christian was a set up, and look how that turned out.

Granny (*in the background*): For goodness sake, this is a different person. Give the guy a chance!

---

[85] "Did she get off the plane?" "I got off the plane!" Hooray! Cheers all around!

[86] Like any rook would do.

[87] Grrr. The cad who misled us all – Marianne especially – in Jane Austen's *Sense and Sensibility*.

[88] That is to say, *Life isn't fair*, as Goldman counsels in his adaptation of *The Princess Bride*.

[89] Lorelei would say it's okay.

Rooks: Uh…

Mom: You might find someone a little faster if you let us help you.

Rooks (*swallowing*): Okay, fine. I'll do it.

Granny (*in the background*): Thank heavens.

Mom: That's my girl.

Dad: Seriously, hon'. What could possibly go wrong?

***

SCENE 39 – Picture Un-Perfect

Rooks is at Food Therapy with her so-called blind date Kirby, the awkward neighbor who lives across the street from her parents.

Michael: I think he likes you.

Rooks and Michael turn from the counter to look at Kirby, who is sitting at the table, rocking back and forth in his chair.

Rooks (*sighing*): I suppose it's a possibility. (*going over to the table and sitting down opposite to him*) Hey, Kirby.

Kirby: I play chess with your father when you're not around.

Rooks: Is that right?

Kirby: Yeah. We play three times a week – sometimes four.

Rooks: Oh. That's nice.

Kirby: You're so pretty.

Rooks: Thank you.

Kirby: No, I mean it. Really pretty.

Rooks: Thank you again.

Kirby: The pictures do not do you justice.

Rooks: The pictures?

Kirby: Yes, the pictures – the ones on the mantle, the ones online.

Kirby pulls out his wallet and starts laying pictures of Rooks on the table one at a time.

Kirby (*holding up a photo*): This one is my favorite.

Michael: Anybody need wa- (*Michael looks at the pictures on the table, and then turns to look at Rooks, who sits with a stunned expression.*) These for the calendar?

Kirby: There's a calendar?

Michael: Not quite, my precious[90] (*He starts to gather the pictures.*)

Kirby: Will I get these back?

Michael: Sure. (*to Rooks*) Hey, are you okay?

Kirby: She's so pretty.

Michael: And sometimes she talks, although I do believe you have done the impossible.

He waves his hand in front of her face.

Michael: Rooks? Hello, Earth to Rooks?

Kirby: I could stand in the bushes and watch her for hours. That's what I usually do when she comes over.

Michael: What self-control!

Kirby: Can you imagine what our children will look like?

Michael: I can't say that I can. Tell you what – while she fills out the restraining order, why don't I get the check?

Rooks (*coming to*): No.

Michael and Kirby: What?

Michael: You want to stay?

Kirby: With me?

---

[90] Oh, Gollum, how we love you!

Rooks: No. (*gently*) Kirby, I'm sorry, but this isn't going to work out.

Thank you, though, for letting me try.

Kirby: Are you sure?

Rooks: I'm sure. Why don't we go and get the check?

They get up to follow Michael to the register. As they walk past the front, Lindsay comes through the doors with Christian.

Rooks (*under her breath*): Oh, dear me. I've entered hell.

Susan: Michael, you've got a call.

Michael leaves to take his call, and Lindsay surveys the situation.

Lindsay: Why, hello, Rooks.

Rooks: Why, hello... Satan.

Lindsay: Bounced back already, I see. (*She walks around Kirby, eyeing him up and down*) Ah, yes. Now this seems about right.

Rooks walks through the double doors and doesn't look back.

***

SCENE 40 – Is This Some Sort of Joke?

There is the build-up, and then there is the breakdown. Rooks is in her car, the tears streaming down her face, as she looks up to the sky to have this conversation.

Rooks: I don't understand. Is this how it's always going to be? Unequal pay in Hollywood[91] and nice girls finish last? 8,423 days[92] of constant Jean Valjean[93] suffering? Because if it is, then I don't get it. I

---

[91] You tell 'em J-Law.
[92] By Fiona's count.
[93] Read it and you will cry. See it and you will cry.

don't understand it at all. What is the purpose of all of this? At some point, aren't I supposed to get ahead? It seems to come together for everyone else. I mean, here I tip my hairdresser. I stop for ducks and turtles and even those annoying little June bugs. I always remember my deodorant. I write my thank yous... Overall, I'm a *pretty nice person*. I hold back a lot. You have no idea. Well, maybe you do. Now, I realize I could work on my traffic skills. They're not so great, but you know, the way I see it, we won't have cars in heaven, so it's not that big a deal. It's not priority, if you know what I mean. Plus, there are a lot of idiots on the road. But I can change, if you want me to... I can stop yelling at those people who don't know how to merge or the ones who ride their brakes every single second. I can do better. (*hitting the steering wheel*) Can nothing come together? Am I forever destined to have the life of some sort of loser? Is that Your plan for me? Because if you want my opinion, that is not the way to inspire confidence. Ah. What am I supposed to learn? (*crying*) And why can't I get any sympathy rain? (*The sprinklers sputter on outside the restaurant.*) Ha, ha. Well, at least You have a sense of humor.[94] I guess I'll take it. (*Rooks picks up her phone to call her mom, only there is no answer.*) Mom? Mom!?! Why don't you answer?

Rooks throws her phone on the passenger seat and puts her head on the steering wheel. After a few minutes, she picks up her phone and tries again. When there is still no answer, she senses something may be awry. She starts her car and heads over to the hospital.

---

[94] It can be hard – sometimes near impossible – to appreciate life's more challenging moments, let alone find the humor. Not everything is Carol-Burnett-Gone-With-The-Wind-Parody kind of funny.

***

SCENE 41 – What Matters Most

Rooks walks quickly through the hospital doors over to reception. She knows something is wrong the minute she sees Rita.

Rooks: Rita. I'm looking for mom. Is she here?

Rita (*with a somber face*): Yeah, she's here baby girl. Down the hall.

Rooks: Down the hall? In Edith's room?

Rita nods her head.

Rooks: Rita? No!

Rita nods again. Rooks rushes down the hall and meets her mom as she is coming out of Edith's room. Her mother's face is stained with tears. Rooks gives her an immediate hug.

Rooks: Mom! Mom! Is it true?

Mom (*barely audible, tears flowing*): I'm afraid so.

Rooks: Mom, I am so sorry. I'm so sorry. What can I do?

Mom: Nothing right now, lovie. Just hold my hand for a few minutes, okay? Then go check on your father. He's in the lobby. (*patting her head*) Her son is on the way.

***

SCENE 42 – Because That's What Families Do

Rooks heads to the lobby to find her dad. Upon meeting, they give each other a big hug.

Rooks: Sorry I walked past you.

Dad: Sorry about your date.

Rooks: I didn't see you.

Dad: He called to tell me.

Rooks: I would've stopped.

Dad: He really is a good guy.

Rooks: I love you, dad.

Dad: And I was just trying to help. I'm glad you were open.

Rooks: I know you were, and I appreciate that.

Dad: That's progress. But I suppose he's not the one for you.

Rooks (*shaking her head*): I'm afraid not. Look, I know you want geographically-proximate grandchildren, but I can't give that to you right now. I don't know when I will. My life seems to have a different story, and we all need to accept that.

Dad (*putting his hand on her cheek*): Rooks, I just want you to be happy. But I don't want you to miss any opportunities, and I don't want you to lose faith.

Rooks: I won't. I promise.

Dad: Or miss any miracles.

Rooks (*pausing*): I hope I don't.

***

SCENE 43 – Mine Eyes = Opened

Rooks leaves her dad in the lobby to go back and check on her mom. When she gets to Edith's doorway, she sees Michael collapsed on his knees at his mother's bedside. Her mother is by his side with her arm wrapped around his shoulders trying to comfort him. Rooks waits and

watches, new tears streaming down her face. Rather than disturb,
Rooks turns and leaves.

***

SCENE 44 – Houston, We Have Arrived

At work, Lindsay and Bruce are in Bruce's office chatting away.

Rooks: Excuse me. May I interrupt?

Lindsay: Do we have a choice?

Bruce: Rooks! Hi. So glad you're here. We wanted to talk to you.

Lindsay: Yes, we did. We wanted to change your hours.

Rooks: Change my hours?

Bruce: So you're here from 7 to 7.

Rooks: Everyday?

Bruce: Except Sundays, of course.

Rooks: But you want me to work Saturdays? We're not even open on Saturday.

Lindsay: It would really help us catch up.

Rooks: On what? My work is finished.

Lindsay: It would help us catch up *on things*.

Rooks: Hmm. So this is a twelve-hour day, six days a week? Install a shower, and I could just live here.

Bruce: We thought you'd be willing. You're pretty low-key. I couldn't pay you anymore, though. According to Lindsay, there's not enough in the budget.

Rooks: How interesting. Um, well, I'm not sure what to say... (*finally, her blessed light bulb moment*) except thank you for the *tremendous* offer.

Bruce: You are welcome.

Rooks: And thank you for the opportunity you've given me to work for you the last few years. I feel I've mastered the advertizing and print world.

Bruce: You have done a tremendous job. What an effort!

Rooks: Yes, I agree. But the time has come for me to move on. Please accept my resignation – effective today.

Lindsay: Today?

Bruce: You're leaving us? You have another job lined up?

Rooks: No, not exactly.

Bruce: Some sort of interview?

Rooks: Not yet.

Bruce: A family business?

Rooks: Not that I know of.

Bruce: Why, that is tremendous! To step into the unknown, without any sort of security. What a giant leap of faith! How exciting! All the best, Rooks.

Rooks turns to go back to the front. Lindsay follows her into the hallway.

Lindsay: Isn't this irresponsible?

Rooks: That depends on your perspective.

Lindsay: What will you do? You can't possibly survive without work.

Rooks: I'm sure I'll find a way. Maybe Richard Hatch[95] has a few suggestions.

Lindsay: So you're going to what? Move in with your parents?

Rooks: It's a possibility. Good thing they like me.

Lindsay: This is ridiculous. You can't leave.

Rooks (*turning to look her square in the face*): But I am.

Lindsay: Is this about Christian? Seriously, as if the two of you could ever be together.

Rooks: Lindsay, you can have him – and whoever else you want. I don't care.

Lindsay: How will this office run without you?

Bruce (*coming out into the hallway*): It's true. We will miss you.

Rooks: Oh, I'm sure you'll be fine – just fine. After all, Lindsay, you've got such tremendous business savvy, not to mention decorating skills, and I – well, you said it yourself – I'm just a secretary.

Rooks grabs her things and heads to the front door. Graham has stepped out into the hallway. Together, the three stand there – Bruce with one arm around Lindsay. He and Graham wave good-bye, as Rooks walks out the front door.

***

SCENE 45 – To Infinity and Beyond[96]

A few weeks have passed. Harper, Denise, and Marley have come to help Rooks pack up her apartment. She has decided to move. She has also made some cookies, albeit on the crunchy side. She leaves one

---

[95] Survivor's first survivor.
[96] Pixar always says it best.

plate on Elisa's doorstep (with a small "thank you"), and another one with her dad (when her mom isn't looking). She takes the third plate with her as she heads over to Food Therapy.

Rooks (*looking toward the sky*): Okay, so I think I get it, and I'm willing to try something new. Just please, please don't let this be awkward.
As she walks to the doors of the restaurant, she runs into Michael coming out.
Rooks: Hey.
Michael: Hi.
Rooks: What are you doing?
Michael: Picking up my last paycheck. I'm about to start medical school.
Rooks: Congratulations, Michael! That's awesome. I know your mom would be proud.
They stare at each other.
Rooks (*clearing her throat*): I brought you some cookies. They're a little crunchy – very different from the ones you make – but I thought you might like them.
Michael (*taking the plate*): Thank you, Rooks. You're pretty sweet, you know that?
Rooks: I'm trying to be.
They walk back toward her car.
Rooks: I'm sorry I didn't stop by sooner. Honestly, I didn't know what to say.
Michael: That's okay. I haven't been here.
Rooks: Right. I'm sorry. I'm sure it's been a rough couple of weeks.

Michael: It has. Well, more like a rough decade, if you know what I mean.

Rooks: I'm pretty sure I do.

Michael: I figured you would. (*They stop at her door.*) You know, we're really not that far behind, if you look at the grand scheme of things.

Rooks: Actually, I've been doing a little thinking about that.

Michael: And?

Rooks: And I think we're right where we're supposed to be. He's got a plan.

Michael: So maybe we could start looking on the flipside?

Rooks: That sounds like a good idea.

They pause.

Rooks (*clearing her throat*): Can I ask you something?

Michael: What's that?

Rooks: Do you think... uh, would it be possible...?

Michael: Yes?

Rooks: Uh, would you go out with me?

Michael: Like on a date?

Rooks: Yeah. On a date.

Michael: Well, I don't know, Rooks.

Rooks: What?

Michael: You realize I'm poor, right? That I'm sorely lacking all those techno gadgets the girls seem to love?

Rooks rolls her eyes.

Michael: I mean it. I just got texting a few months ago.

Rooks: Ah, catching up to the rest of the world, are you?

Michael: And food? Well, let's just say it's Ramen[97] from here on out.

Rooks: And crunchy cookies.

Michael: And crunchy cookies. (*He sets the cookie plate on the hood.*)
Seriously, though, Rooks, I'm not that far in life.

Rooks: Too many curveballs?

Michael (*laughing*): Not to mention a few screw ones. (*taking a deep breath*) Still want to go out with me?

Rooks: Yeah. I do.

Michael: And date me?

Rooks: Yes. Yes, I do.

Michael: Yeah? Really? That's good.... Real good... Because you're *soooooo* pretty....

Rooks starts to punch him, but Michael grabs her arm and pulls her in to kiss instead.

~~The End~~

The Beginning

***

---

[97] What? One package is now 24 cents? Blast that Zayn, and blast inflation!

Doraina Pyle is a firm believer of self-improvement and living simply. Much of her time is spent trying to "Make a positive difference" as a volunteer at church and in the community. In 2003, she earned a Dual Bachelor's degree in French Studies and English Composition from the University of North Texas. In 2009, she completed a Masters in Language Acquisition and Teaching at Brigham Young University. In her spare time, Doraina enjoys reading, dancing, piano, and travel. Her previous works include *My Mid-Single Mindset* and *The Parable of the Weedy Yard*.

For more information, please visit www.DorainaPyle.com

www.ingramcontent.com/pod-product-compliance
Lightning Source LLC
Chambersburg PA
CBHW070523130626

46555CB00003B/1318